W9-BRG-570

First published in Japan in 2013 by Child Honsha Co., Ltd. under the title *999-hiki no kyôdai no Otouto*.
First published in the United States and Canada in 2015 by NorthSouth Books Inc., an imprint of NordSüd Verlag AG, CH-8005 Zürich, Switzerland.
English language translation rights arranged with Child Honsha Co., Ltd through Japan Foreign-Rights Center.
Distributed in the United States by NorthSouth Books Inc., New York 10016.

Library of Congress Cataloging-in-Publication Data is available.
Printed in Latvia by Livonia Print, Riga, October 2014.
ISBN: 978-0-7358-4202-1

1 3 5 7 9 • 10 8 6 4 2

www.northsouth.com

Ken Kimura · Yasunari Murakami

999 FROGS

AND A LITTLE BROTHER

North
South

It was spring. At the edge of the big big pond, 999 tadpole brothers were playing together.

999 tadpoles were doing well.

998 tadpoles sprouted legs.

Only the tadpole born last didn't have his legs yet.

"Wait!" the little tadpole shouted as he tried to catch up with the others.

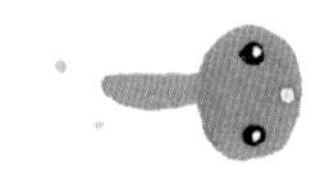

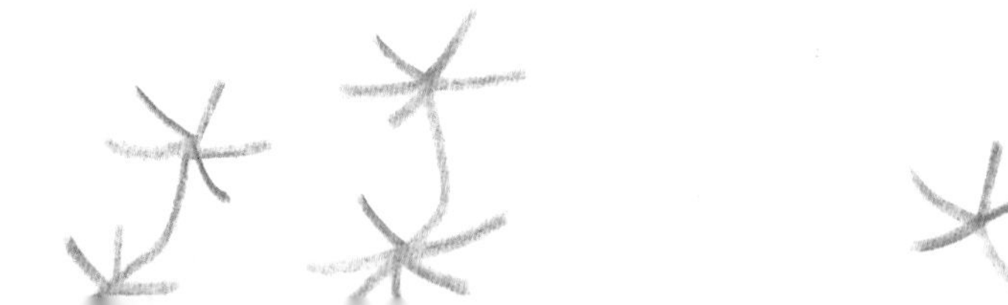

998 tadpoles sprouted arms.

998 tadpoles swam fast.

Only the tadpole born last didn't have his arms yet.

"Wait!" the little tadpole shouted as he tried to catch up with the others.

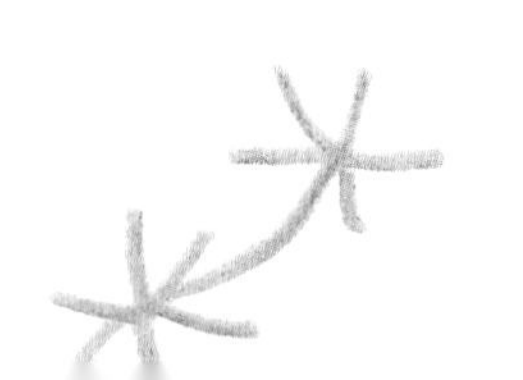

998 tadpoles became frogs.

JUMP! JUMP! JUMP!

998 frogs jumped out of the pond.

But the tadpole born last hadn't lost his tail yet. He couldn't follow his bigger brothers.

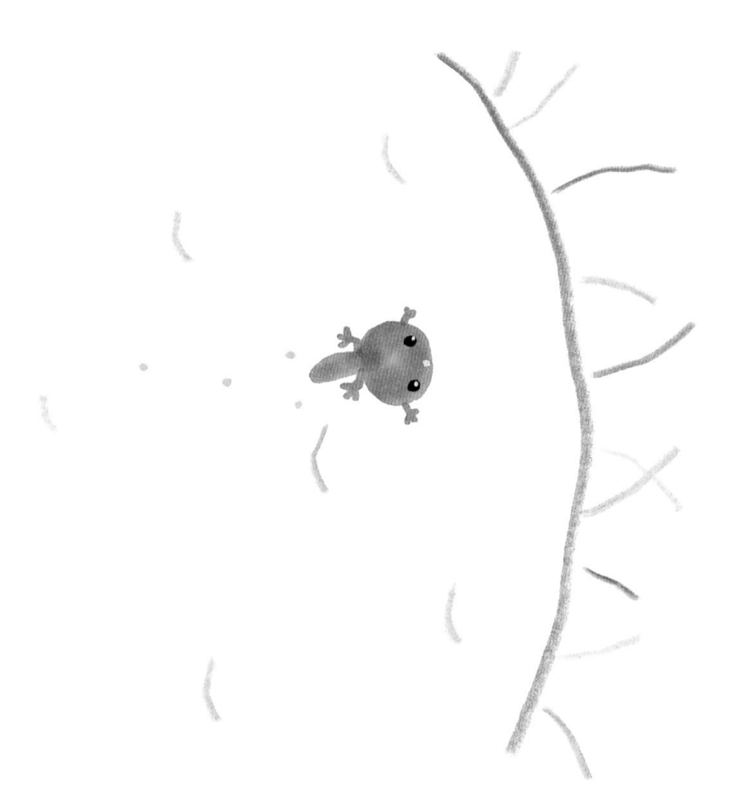

"Lucky them! I want to leave the pond too!" said the little tadpole.

He watched them hop away, when all of a sudden . . .

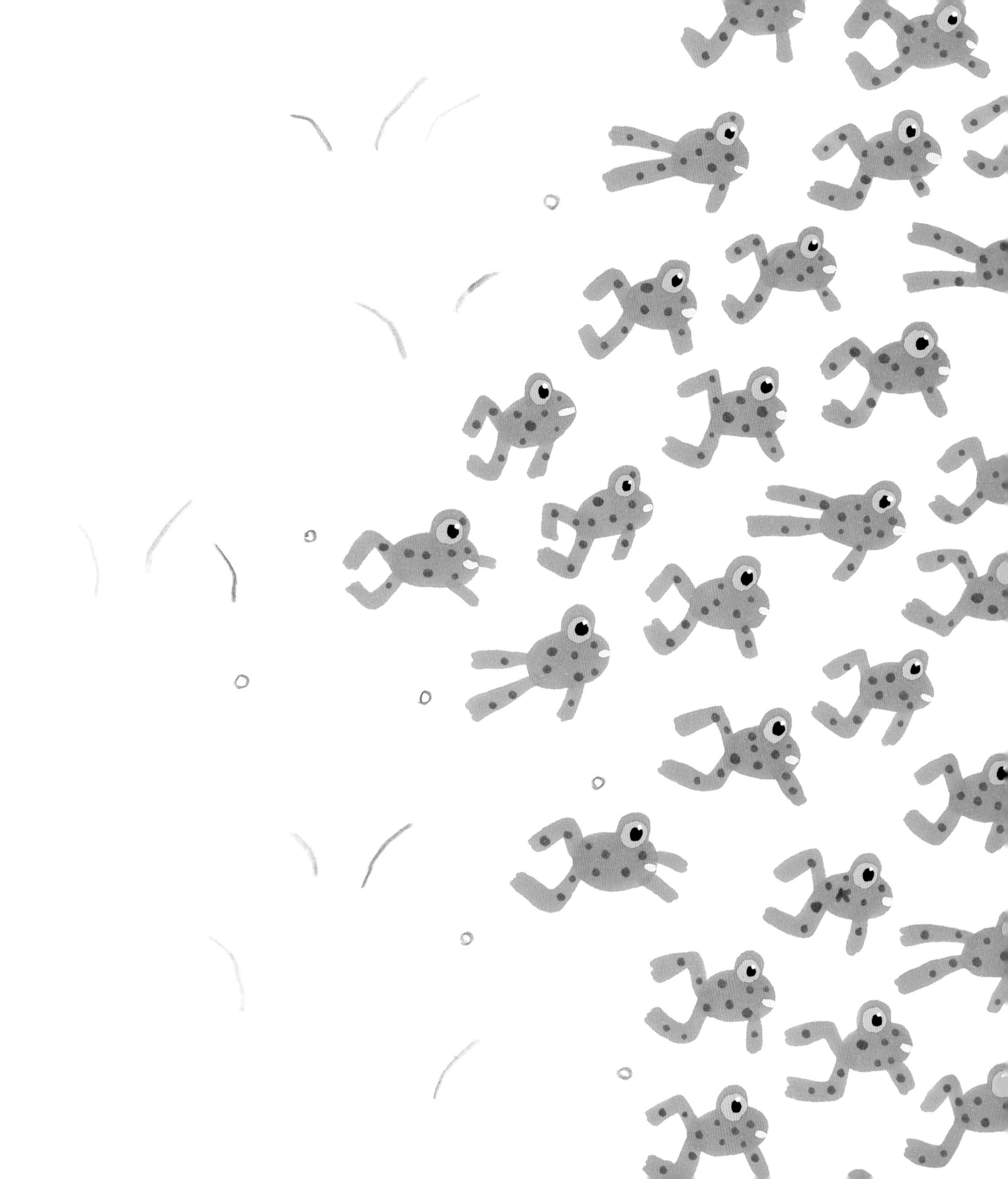

. . . a small voice said, “Big Brother!”

“Are you calling *me* Big Brother?” asked the little tadpole.

“Yes, I am. You have a tail and you have legs. Aren’t you my big brother?” the baby animal asked.

The little tadpole was very pleased. “Yes, I am your big brother. Let’s play together!”

First they played hide-and-seek.

"You hide and I'll try to find you. Are you ready?" asked Big Brother.

"Yes," said Little Brother. "Catch me if you can!"

"Hmm, where could he be?"

Now it was Little Brother's turn to seek.
Big Brother got caught very quickly.
"I saw your tail! You're very easy to find, Big Brother!"
The two of them played all day.

That night they slept side by side.

ZZZZZZzzzzzz!

Until a big crayfish showed up . . .

"There you are! I've been looking for you everywhere," she said.

Little Brother woke up and whispered, "Mommy!"

Then Little Brother crawled away with his mother.

When Big Brother woke up the next morning, Little Brother was gone.

"Where's my little brother?" he said as he looked all around.

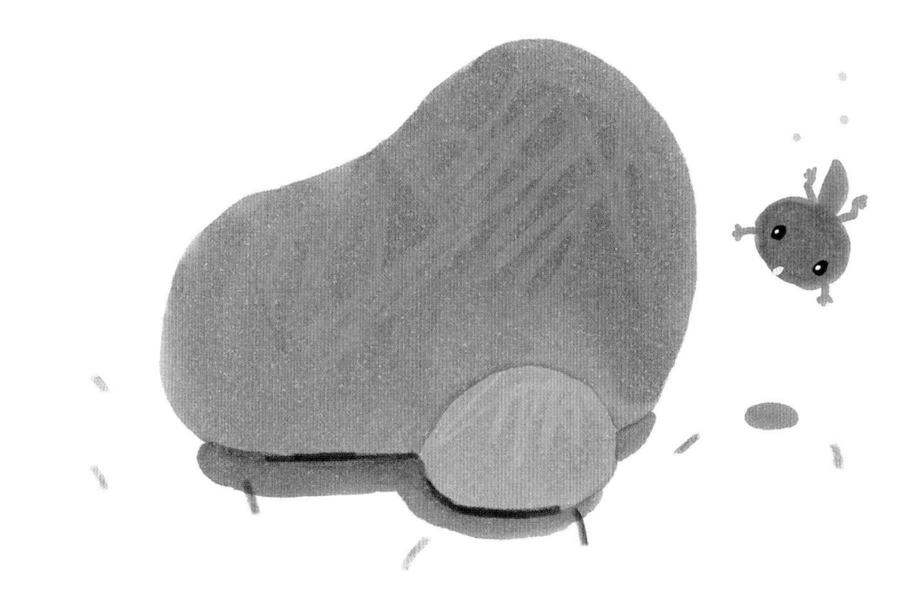

“He’s not here . . .

“. . . and he’s not here either. Where could he be?”

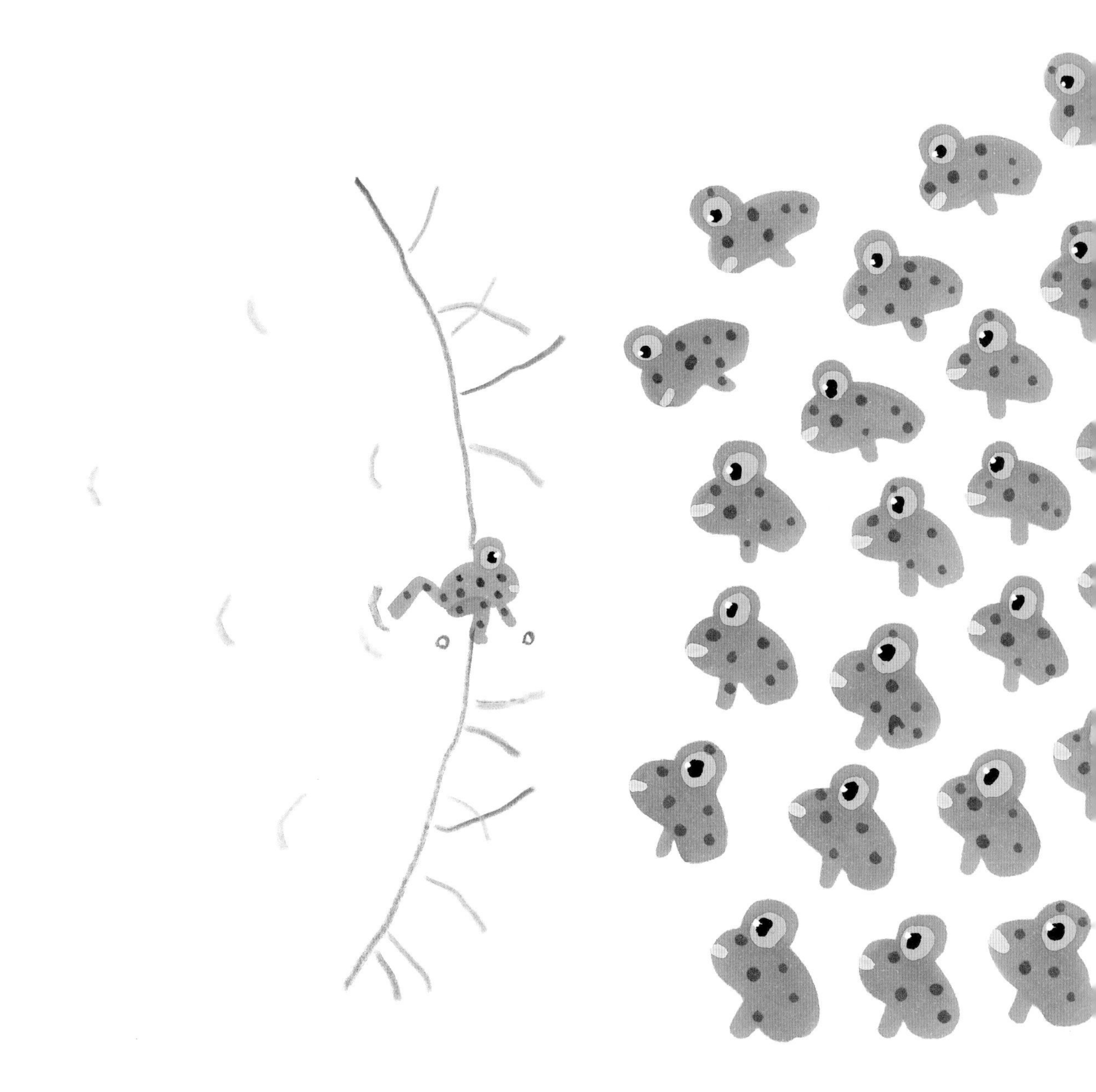

Big Brother looked and looked. After a few days, he finally became a frog. But he still kept looking for Little Brother.

"Maybe he left the pond."

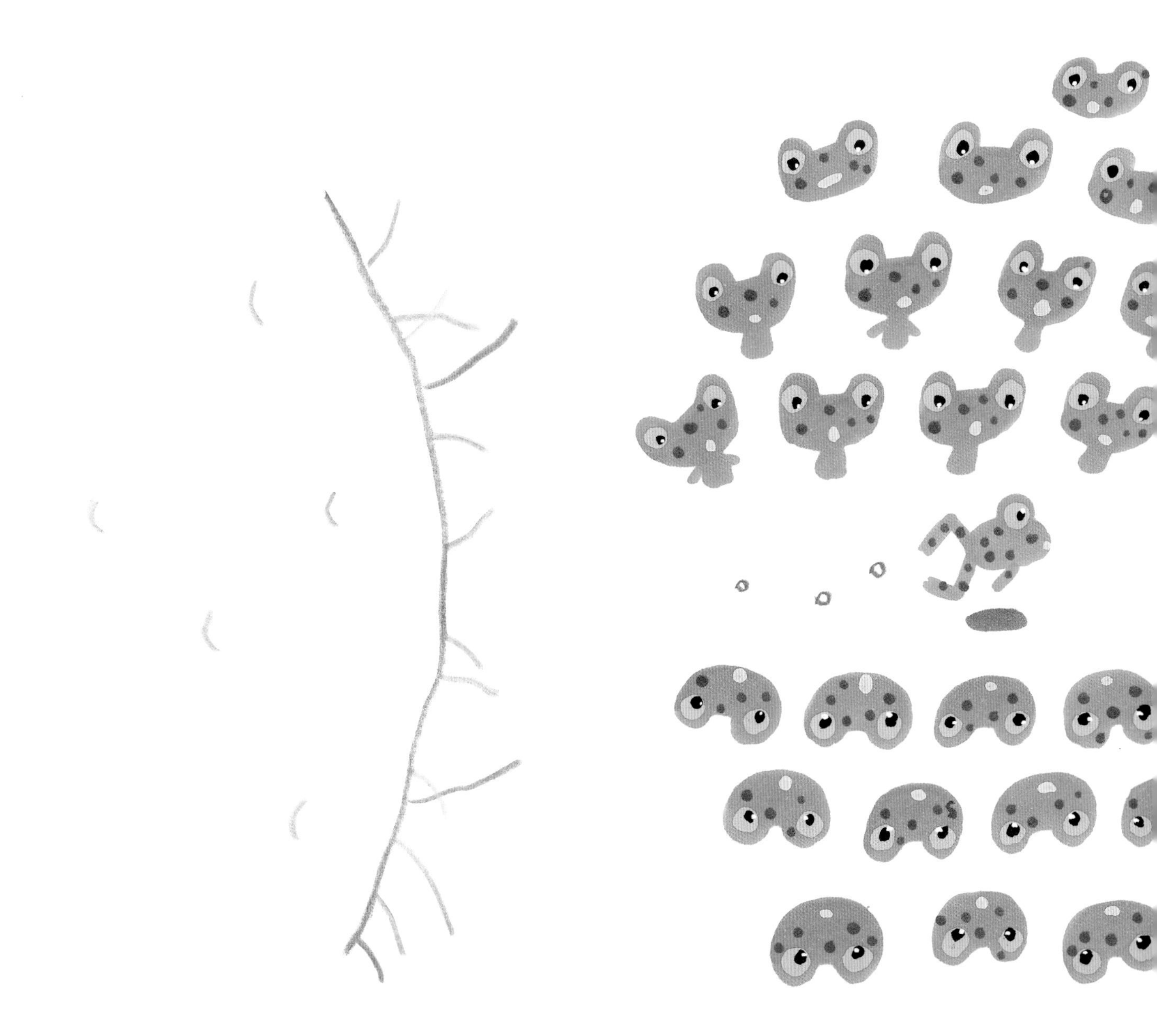

Big Brother jumped out of the water and hopped by his brothers. He heard a rustling in the long reeds.

"Ah, maybe he's here. I found you!" said Big Brother, jumping into the grass.

But it wasn't Little Brother. It was a BIG snake!

"What a yummy-looking frog! I'm gonna taste it," said the snake.

Big Brother was terrified.

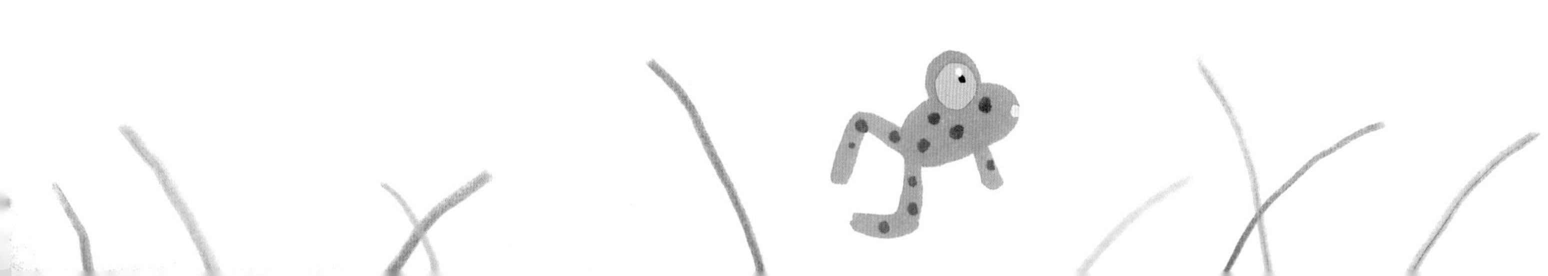

"PLEASE! HELP!" he shouted, and jumped back into the pond.

"I'm not going to let my dinner escape. Come back!" said the snake.

But at that moment . . .

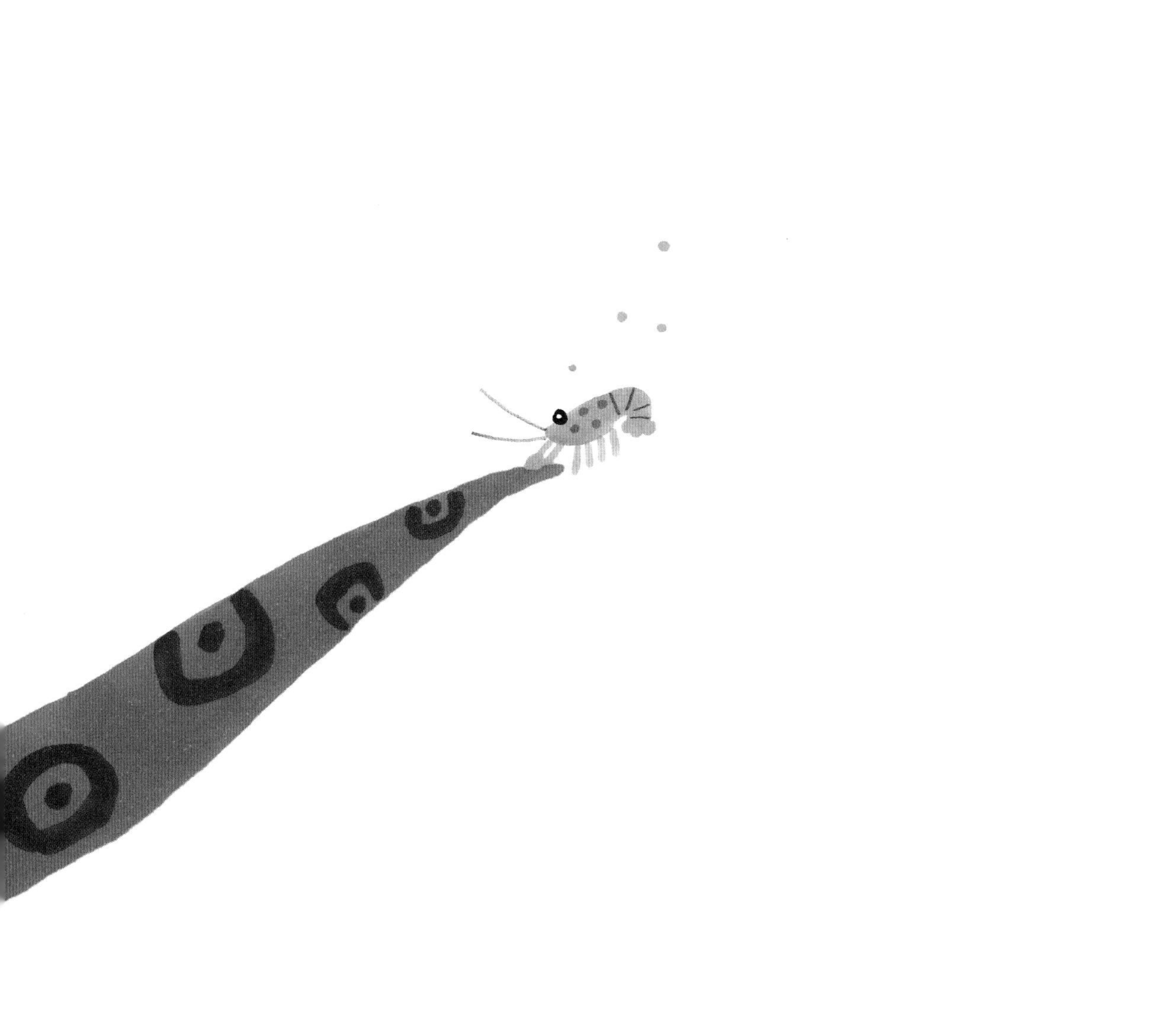

. . . a small voice shouted, "STOP IT!"
A little crayfish grabbed the snake's tail.

“What are you doing? Don’t disturb me!” said the snake, whipping his tail.

The little crayfish was catapulted up in the air.

"AAAGH!"

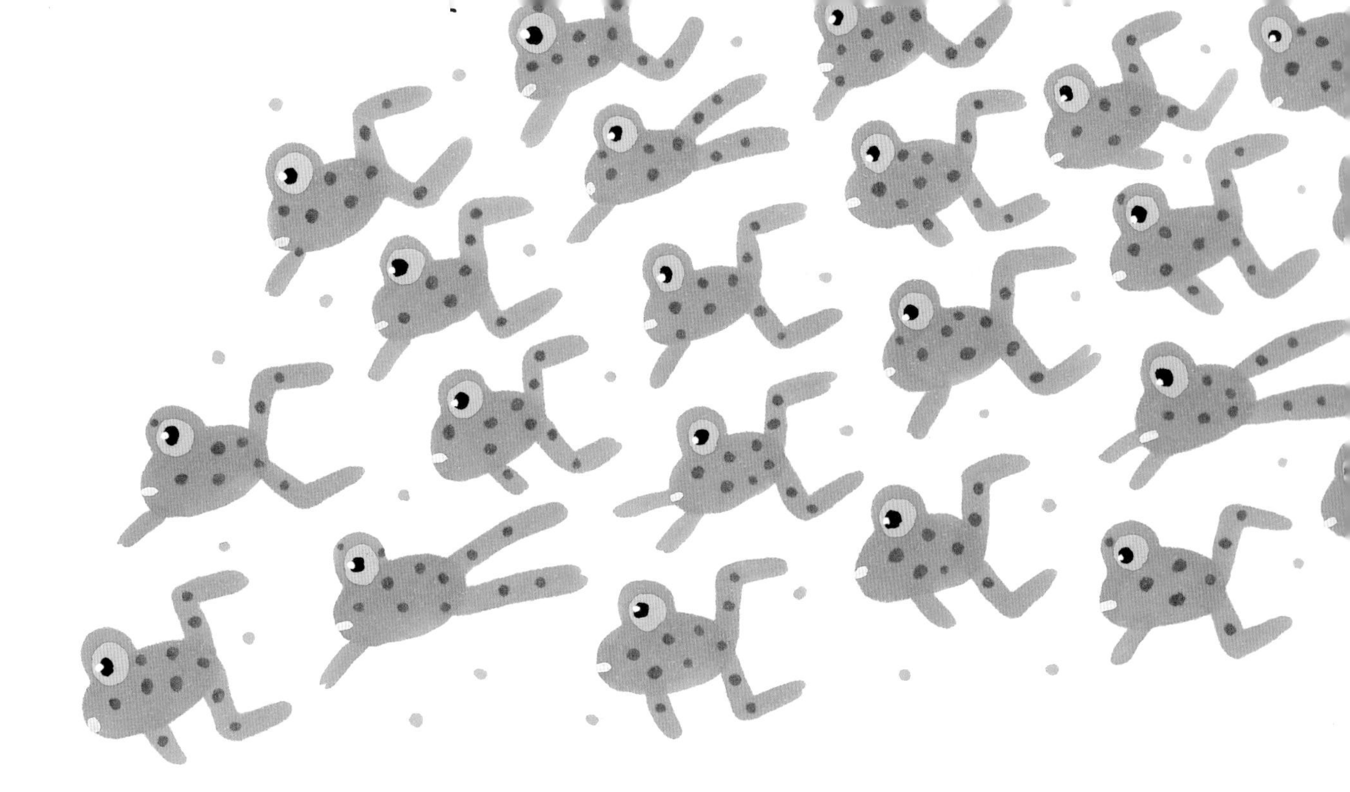

Big Brother's 998 brothers hurried over to help.
"Quickly! We have to help our brother!"

"HEAVE-HO! HEAVE-HO!"

They pulled with all of their might, but the snake was strong. Very strong!

He dragged them all over the ground.

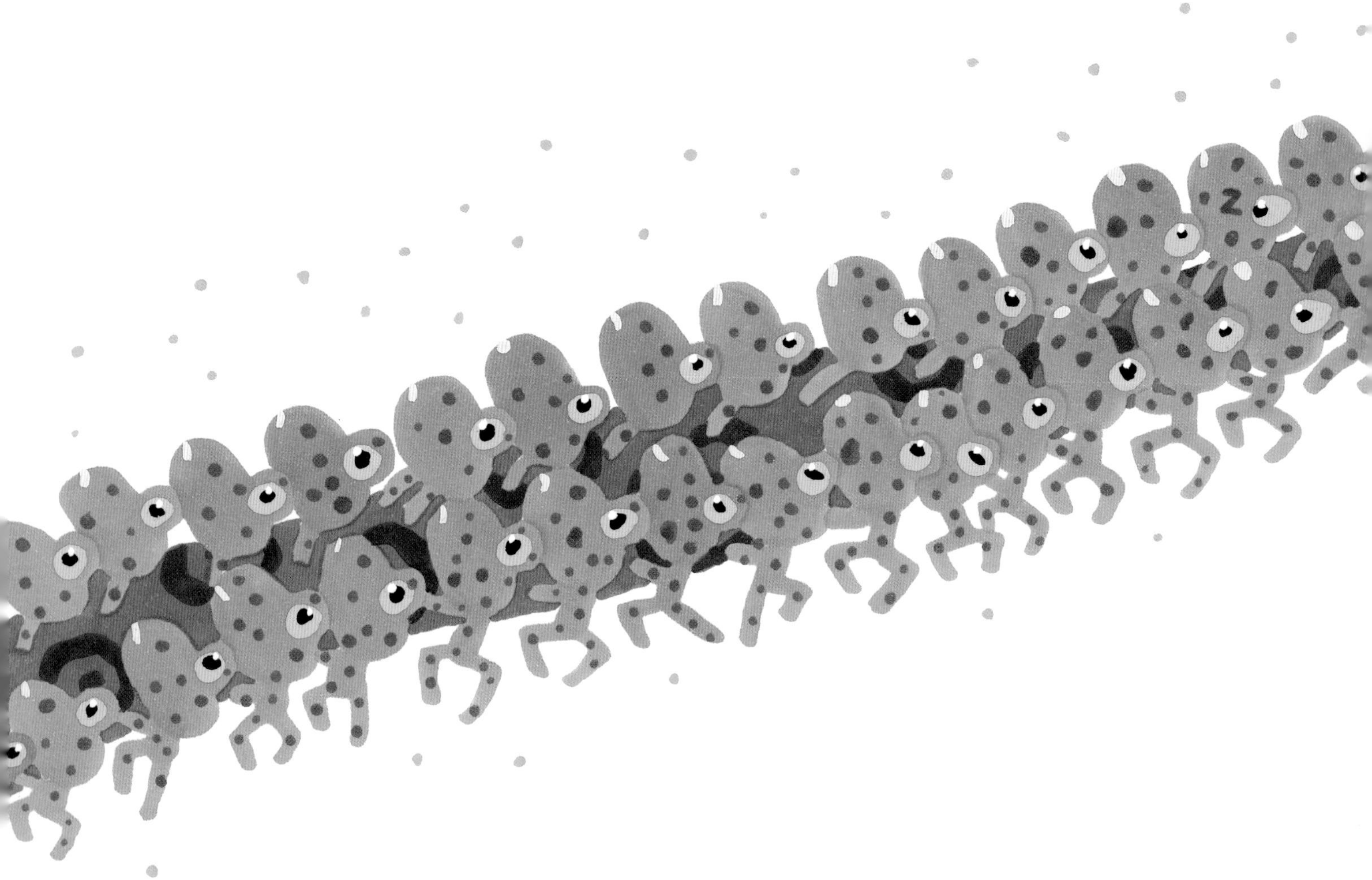

Until a big crayfish came . . .

SNAP!

"What did you do to my little boy!" the big crayfish scolded, and grabbed the snake's tail with her pincers.

"Ouch! That hurt!" the snake said as he hurried out of the pond.

"Hooray! We defeated the snake!" the frogs cheered.

“Thanks for your help!” the 999 frog brothers said to the little crayfish.

“You’re Big Brother, aren’t you? I recognized you right away. You’re still very bad at hiding,” the little crayfish said.

“Little Brother! It’s you! You helped me!” Big Brother said with a smile.

"Okay, but now we have to go. Thanks for being so nice to my little boy," mother crayfish said.

"Bye-bye, Big Brother! Stay healthy!"

"You too, Little Brother! Stay safe!"

Little Brother and his mother went home.

999 frogs sing together every day:

RIBBIT! RIBBIT! RIBBIT!

Big Brother sings too. From time to time he thinks of his little brother. And what a great time they had together.